I AM HIDING

BY MERCER MAYER

Random House 🏠 New York

Library of Congress Catalog Card Number: 94-68290   ISBN 0-679-87347-3
Manufactured in Italy   10 9 8 7 6 5 4 3 2 1
🐸 GREEN FROG PUBLISHERS, INC. / J. R. SANSEVERE BOOK

I am swinging.

I am hearing.

I am leaving.

I am hiding!

I am peeking.

I am climbing.

I am waiting.

I am jumping.

I am creeping.

I am hopping.

I am running.

I am looking.

I am pushing.

I am crawling.

I am resting.

I am spying.

I am hiding again.

I am sneezing.

I am caught!